Dear Parent:
Your child's love of reading starts here!

Every child learns to read in a different way and at his or her own speed. Some go back and forth between reading levels and read favorite books again and again. Others read through each level in order. You can help your young reader improve and become more confident by encouraging his or her own interests and abilities. From books your child reads with you to the first books he or she reads alone, there are I Can Read Books for every stage of reading:

SHARED READING
Basic language, word repetition, and whimsical illustrations, ideal for sharing with your emergent reader

BEGINNING READING
Short sentences, familiar words, and simple concepts for children eager to read on their own

READING WITH HELP
Engaging stories, longer sentences, and language play for developing readers

READING ALONE
Complex plots, challenging vocabulary, and high-interest topics for the independent reader

ADVANCED READING
Short paragraphs, chapters, and exciting themes for the perfect bridge to chapter books

I Can Read Books have introduced children to the joy of reading since 1957. Featuring award-winning authors and illustrators and a fabulous cast of beloved characters, I Can Read Books set the standard for beginning readers.

A lifetime of discovery begins with the magical words **"I Can Read!"**

*Visit www.icanread.com for information
on enriching your child's reading experience.*

I Can Read Book® is a trademark of HarperCollins Publishers.
Balzer + Bray is an imprint of HarperCollins Publishers.

Louise and the Class Pet
Copyright © 2018 by Kelly Light
All rights reserved. Manufactured in U.S.A.
No part of this book may be used or reproduced in any manner whatsoever without
written permission except in the case of brief quotations embodied in critical
articles and reviews. For information address HarperCollins Children's Books,
a division of HarperCollins Publishers, 195 Broadway, New York, NY 10007.
www.icanread.com

ISBN 978-0-06-236368-8 (pbk.bdg.) — ISBN 978-0-06-236369-5 (trade bdg.)

The artist used many black Prismacolor pencils and Photoshop to create the
illustrations for this book.

18 19 20 21 22 LSCC 10 9 8 7 6 5 4 3 2 1 ❖ First Edition

I Can Read!™

BEGINNING
1
READING

LOUISE
and the
Class Pet

Story by Laura Driscoll
Pictures by Kelly Light

BALZER & BRAY
An Imprint of HarperCollinsPublishers

This is going to be
the best weekend ever!

I have a friend
staying over.

This friend is super sweet.

This friend is super cute.

This friend is warm

and cuddly

and . . . furry.

It is our class pet—
a guinea pig!
Finally it is my turn
to take care of him
for the weekend.

His name is Pigcasso.

Like the artist Picasso!

So you must love art.

Right, Pigcasso?

This is my room.

See?

I love art, too!

Hmmm.

I think you need
some art for your cage.
Maybe a Pigcasso portrait?

Aww.

What is it, Pigcasso?

Are you hungry?

Oh, poor Pigcasso.

Are you thirsty?

SQUEAK!

Pigcasso?!

What is the matter?

Are you okay?

What did you do
to scare Pigcasso?

Don't worry, Pigcasso.

I won't let the cat hurt you.

Here, Art.

You hold Pigcasso

while I make his cage cozy.

Pigcasso?

Pigcasso!

Where did he go?

Come out, Pigcasso.

Here, boy.

There he is!

No, over there!

Art!

This is no time to play!

We need to find Pigcasso!

Oh, wow!

You found him!

Nice job, Art!

There you go, Pigcasso!

That's better.

Isn't it?